I0646759

This book is dedicated to the following:

The staff and guides on Adventure Canada's
Into the Northwest Passage, 2018.

The Captain and Crew of Ocean Endeavor, 2018.

The Inuit People of Greenland, and the Nunavut Territory
who welcomed us as visitors to their land.

Cedar and Jason for allowing me to transform
cabin 5142 from a place of rest into an artist studio,
a place to paint and process all the wonders of this trip.

And my husband, Jerry, your support makes it all possible.

Red Cinder Press
243 Jersey Street, San Francisco, CA 94114
helenchellin.com

Available through the artist and Amazon.com.

Published 2019 – Red Cinder Press © 2019 by Helen Chellin.

ISBN 978-0-9888875-5-8

You Can't Make a Mistake in the Arctic

Adventure Into the Northwest Passage
GREENLAND & CANADIAN ARCTIC

Paintings by
Helen Chellin

Book Design by
Amy Reilly

"Come my friends, it is not too late to seek

new worlds. Push off and sitting well in order smite.

The sounding furrows, for my purpose holds."

Alfred Lord Tennyson, from Ulysses

Blue Bear in an Overcoat

Change of Coats

Excited and a bit nervous, Blue Bear leaves

San Francisco for the Toronto Airport. At the Toronto Sheraton Gateway

Hotel, a welcome and an orientation meeting was held. Early the next

morning, the group leaves by charter to Airport Kangerlussuaq, Greenland.

Ocean Endeavor at Harbor Dock — Sisimiut, Greenland

Leaving Toronto –
Arriving Greenland

Walking into Sisimiut

Inuit Woman

Inuit Woman Gathering Arctic Cotton

Birdwatching

Arctic Landscape

Beginning Hike

In Conversation with Suzanne

Two Points of View

Zodiac Driver with Passengers

"Travel is fatal to prejudices,
bigotry and narrow-mindedness."

Mark Twain

"**There are no foreign lands.**

It is only the traveller who is foreign."

Robert Louis Stevenson

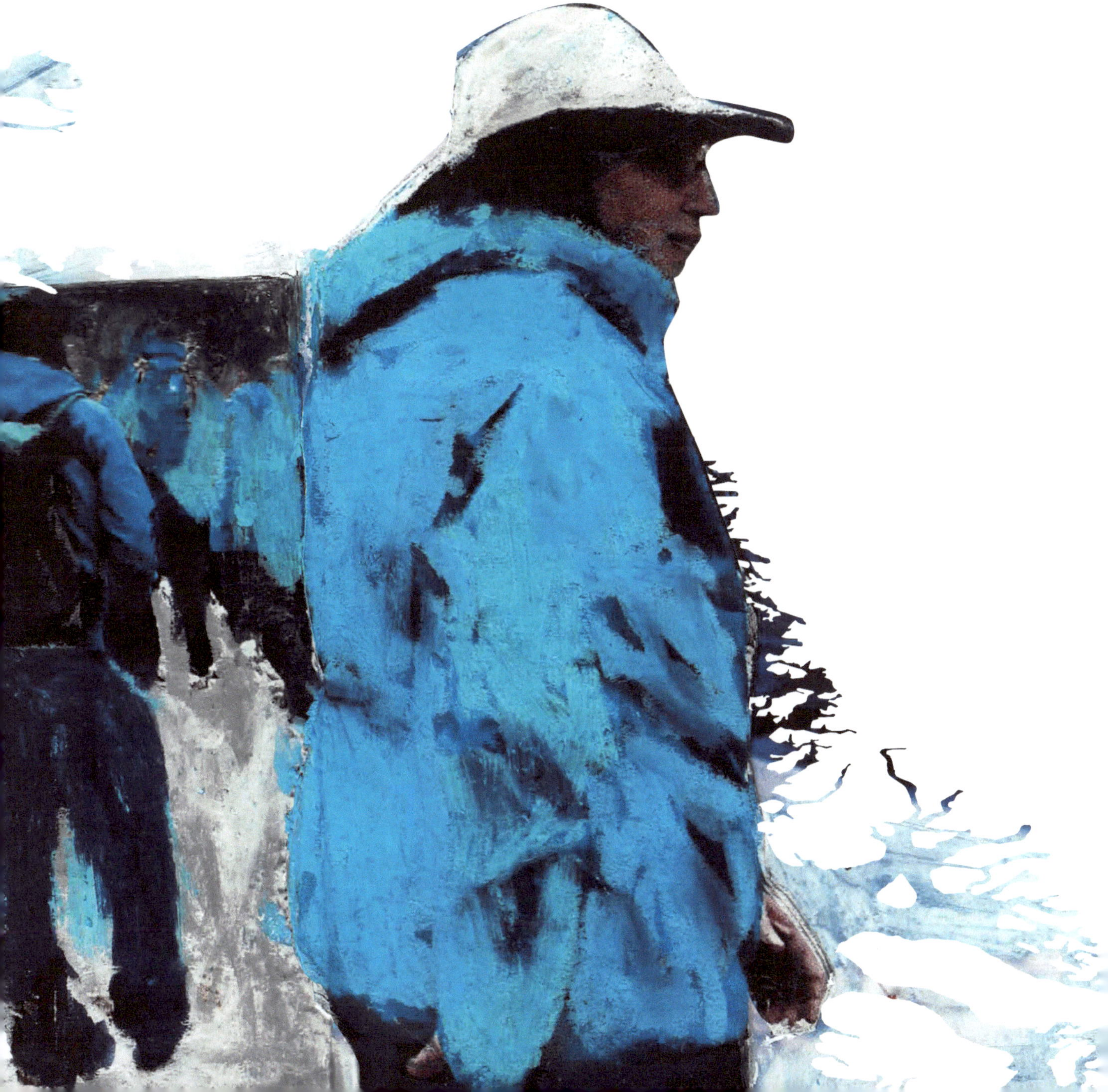

Long Hike Across Sea Ice

One Bear – Two Hikers

In tandem with the polar sea, the Ocean Endeavor,

weaved; through an archipelago of earthened rock and ice;

truly a floating world.

We crossed the Davis Strait to the Canadian Arctic,

landed in Qikiqtarjuag, and continued the journey towards

Neddluysiaq Fjord, Auyuittaq National Park.

Conversation

Out For a Ride

Arctic Explorers

As a visitor to this land and sea, I joined the

expedition with the intention to paint and open myself

up to this beauty. Transit through the Northwest Passage

changes the perception of time, and I often felt as though

I was continuously floating in a dream-like state.

Looking Back

"And if we were not annihilated by the contemplation of such vast adventure it was by grace of that wise providence of man's nature which, to preserve his reason, lets him be thoughtless before immensity."

Rockwell Kent

Gjoa-Roald Amandsen, 1906 – First to sail through the North West Passage

Ocean Endeavor Sailing Polar Sea by Infinity Pool

The Henry Larsen – Canadian Ice Breaker

Ships on the Polar Sea

Arctic Transit

"If a writer knows enough about what he is writing about, he may omit things that he knows. The dignity of movement of an iceberg is due to only one ninth of it being above water."

Ernest Hemingway

"There is nothing, absolutely nothing
half so much fun worth doing as simply
messing around in boats."

Kenneth Grahame,
The Wind in the Willows

Out on the Water

Dreaming of Zodiac Rides

"You can't make a mistake in the Arctic," our Zodiac driver cautioned.

Seated in the Zodiac, passengers armed with cameras explore sea ice, calving icebergs from arctic glaciers, and marine mammals. Riding low on the surface of the sea, the vast open space made us all feel so miniscule in comparison to the epic scale of the Arctic world. This new perspective accentuated the dynamics of the ocean, and I felt as though I became part of the sea itself, standing still only upon anchoring our vessel.

Zodiac in Ice and Shimmering Water

Zodiac Ride

Zodiac with Sea Ice and Glacier

Zodiac Tour

Alone on the Red Waters

Kayaking in Blues and Greens

Sue on Hike

Two by Land – Two by Sea

Flying Over Water

To Tall Ships, High Winds, and Polar Bears

"Life is about change,

sometimes its painful,

sometimes its beautiful.

But most of the time its both."

Lana Lang

White Light Aerial View

Sea Ice – Two Mountains – Blue Sky

At times, I awoke at night from the sound of the hull scraping against underwater ice; and each morning, our expedition leader, Jason, would recite a literary quote, a current ice report, location coordinates and the upcoming schedule over the intercom to all passengers and crew. I grew to wake up each day smiling.

Scaffold as Portal

Group of Portals on Glacier

Arctic Layering

Side View

Arctic Cairns

Inuit Home – High Arctic

Hidden in the Blue Hour

Arctic Whites and Blues

"If there is magic on this planet, it is contained
in water. It's substance reaches everywhere; it touches
the past and prepares the future."

Loren Eisely

Shaman as Bear

Polar Bear Walking

Alone on the Ice

Opposite Page : Polar Bear on Ice Step

Polar Bear Moves Across Sea Ice

Strong Winds – Strong Bear

Polar Bear Resting On the Ice

There Were Three Bears

Blue Bear

Ursus maritimus

Sleeping White Bear

Sleeping Blue Bear

Ancestors

Opposite page – Cairns Awaken in Blue Hour

Arctic Waves

Coming and Going

"The land returns an identity of its own,
still deeper and more subtle than we can know.
Our obligation towards it then becomes simple;
To approach with an uncalculating mind
and an attitude of regard."

Barry Lopez

Blue Caribou

Caribou with Mountain

Hunting on Ice

Travel by Land

Arctic Migration

Blue Hour Animals

"This grand show is eternal. It is always sunrise somewhere; the dew is never all dried at once; a shower is forever falling; vapor ever rising. Eternal sunrise, eternal sunset, eternal dawn and gloaming, on seas and continents and islands, each in its turn, as the round earth rolls. And for this we are forever grateful."

John Muir

Ancestors in the Northern Lights

Breaking Bread – Sharing Cultures

Following pages – To Bear Witness, (detail) acrylic on unstretched canvas, 5' x 7.'

Cheers! L'Chaim!

Artist Statement

The brown bear moved out of the forests during the last ice age and became a subspecies known as the polar bear. This white bear is now moving again because of climate change that has mostly been caused by humans. Both of our species face possible extinction if we do not bear witness to this fact. This past year I travelled to the high arctic by ship, the Ocean Endeavor. I moved in tandem with the polar sea weaving through an archipelago containing many islands of earth and ice. The Canadian arctic is a floating world. It is land that has many ways to record time. The ice cores and glaciers record time past and then melt into the present. Going to the arctic I am a visual recorder of time in my paintings. Like the ocean and ice, my images expand and recede; in and out of spatial realms, like the polar bear moves between land, ocean and ice. Included in the paintings are portals defined by contour line. They appear two-dimensional. They are not. The passengers of this expedition, native peoples, and marine animals sometimes move together through these portals. Often all three are not in tandem. The painted portals are a way I travel with them.

About the Artist

Living on a Hawaiian Island where creativity is set on fire changed how I perceived the world around me. I was born in Brooklyn. My paintings and artist books tell stories about how the forces of nature and culture are brought together. It is especially true now when human activity plays a large part in the cause of rapid climate change.

On the Big Island of Hawaii I founded the Red Cinder Creativity Center and was the director of this artist-in-residency program until it closed in 2012.

I was an artist-in-residence at the The Cité Internationale des arts Paris and the de Young Museum in San Francisco and received a State of California Arts Council grant as a teaching artist.

In 2008 I created Tsunami: The Great Wave of Plastic Pollution. This was a science and art installation and performance at the Army Corp of Engineers Bay Model in Sausalito, California.

At 455 Market Street in San Francisco, I had a one person show titled Toxic Beauty using marine debris plastics collected at South Point Beach in Hawaii.

In 2009, my work about volcanoes was shown at a USGS Open House in Menlo Park in an exhibit called The Art in Science as well as at Harvard University in an exhibit titled Runaway Nature. I completed a painting series titled One Hundred Views of Kilauea Volcano. The first fifty paintings in this series were exhibited at the Wailoa Arts and Cultural Center in Hilo, Hawaii in October 2013.

In 2014, I participated in the 50/50 Show at the Sanchez Art Center in Pacifca, California, building on images from The Art of Arranging Japanese Volcanoes series.
Dec. 2016 my work was viewed in a group show at the Canessa Gallery in San Francisco

More artwork and books at **helenchellin.com** or email **hchellin@gmail.com.**